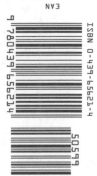

EAN

ISBN 0-439-65621-4

9 780439 656214

50599

STATIC SHOCK™

DOUBLE TROUBLE

Adapted by
Tracey West

As Seen on WB KIDS

SCHOLASTIC

DOUBLE TROUBLE

DOUBLE TROUBLE

by Tracey West

**Based on the teleplays
"Grounded" by Len Uhley
and
"Replay" by Len Uhley and
Brooks Wachtel**

SCHOLASTIC INC.
New York   Toronto   London   Auckland   Sydney
Mexico City   New Delhi   Hong Kong   Buenos Aires

ISBN 0-439-65621-4

© 2004 Milestone Media, Inc. All rights reserved. Static Shock and all related characters and elements are trademarks of DC Comics. WB Shield and Kids' WB logo: TM & © Warner Bros. Entertainment, Inc.

Published by Scholastic Inc. All rights reserved. SCHOLASTIC and associated logos are trademarks and/or registered trademarks of Scholastic Inc.

12 11 10 9 8 7 6 5 4 3 2   4 5 6 7 8 9/0

Printed in the U.S.A.   40
First printing, September 2004

What's Up With Virgil?

Virgil Hawkins used to be just like everybody else. He went to school, hung out with his buddy, Richie, got yelled at by his dad, and got into fights with his big sister.

Then one day Virgil found himself in the wrong place at the wrong time. He got caught in a chemical explosion. A Big Bang. Everyone hit by the chemical ended up changing — in a big way. They became more than human. That's why they're called meta-humans. Each meta-human ended up with a different power.

After the Big Bang, Virgil found out he could

control static electricity. He could light up a whole city block with one energy blast. He could make metal bend, twist, or fly through the air.

Each meta-human had a different power. Unfortunately, most meta-humans decided to use their powers to cause trouble. But not Virgil. He decided to use his powers to become a super hero instead.

Richie helped him out. He hooked Virgil up with super hero gear like cool threads, and a metal disk Virgil could use to surf the sky.

That's how Virgil became the super hero called Static. Get ready to watch him in action. It'll be a real shock to your system!

CHAPTER ONE
What Is That Thing?

Dakota City isn't a bad place to live. Most days, it's safe for anyone, young or old, to walk down the street.

But today wasn't one of those days.

A gray-haired woman stepped out of Mr. Green's grocery store. She carried a heavy shopping bag in her arms. Her purse hung over her shoulder.

A man came up behind her, yanked the purse off her arm, and ran away.

"Help!" screamed the woman.

Almost instantly, a voice yelled, "Yo, buddy!

Don't you have anything better to do than pick on a nice old lady?"

The thief looked up, startled. Floating above his head was a boy in a long, black and purple coat. His dreadlocks waved on top of his head. He was standing on a round metal disk.

"Name's Static," he told the shocked robber. "Now, if you don't mind, I'll take back that purse."

Static aimed an electric charge at the metal clasp on the purse and it immediately fell off the robber's arm. Static held the charge and moved the purse through the air, back into the old woman's arms.

"Thank you, son," she replied, smiling.

"No problem," Static said. Then he heard the sound of running footsteps and turned. The mugger was tearing down the street.

Static shook his head. "That's not very nice. He didn't even say good-bye!"

Static flew after the robber, who had hopped a fence into a nearby construction site. Static quickly flew over the fence.

There was no sign of the perp, just a big crane with a demolition ball hanging from it, and a huge, empty pit. Where had the robber gone?

Suddenly, Static heard a groaning sound. He turned toward the crane as the robber's head poked up from the driver's seat. He was grinning. Before Static could react, the man swung the demolition ball right at him! It slammed into Static's disk, and he fell right into the bottom of a muddy pit. His head was spinning.

The robber leaned over the pit and smiled.

"You meta-humans think you rule this city," he crowed. "Well, think again!"

The robber grabbed a crowbar. He jumped into the pit and charged at Static.

Static jumped to his feet, but the ground beneath him began to move, almost knocking him over again. The robber stopped in his tracks.

"What's that?" Static asked. "An earthquake?"

The ground kept shaking. Static watched as a blob of mud rose up behind the robber. It rose higher and higher.

Then the mud fell off to reveal a huge creature! It looked like some kind of giant germ! It waved its stringlike arms and made a weird groaning sound.

"Definitely *not* an earthquake!" Static said.

CHAPTER TWO
Goopzilla!

One of the creature's stringy arms reached down and grabbed the thief. Slimy green glop dripped from the monster and landed on the robber's skin.

"Ow! It burns!" he screamed.

The robber was a real creep, but Static couldn't stand by and let him get hurt by this giant slime creature.

He quickly scanned the pit. A coil of metal cable was curled up nearby. Static zapped it with his electric powers and the coil floated up and whipped around the robber. Static used his powers to give the coil a yank, pulling the robber free. The robber fell onto the dirt as the creature let out a loud, angry roar.

Zap! Zap! Zap! Static blasted the creature with one energy bolt after another. It let out another wail, and then sank back down into the mud.

Static stopped. Had he beaten the creature? He wasn't sure, but he wasn't about to go digging in the mud to find out.

Besides, he had another mess to take care of. Static raised his flying disk in the air and hopped onto it. Then he zapped the metal cable, which was still tied around the robber, and lifted the man into the air.

"I'll drop you off at the police station on my way home," Static told him.

The robber glared at him.

"Hey, you should thank me," Static said. "I don't let just anybody ride around Static-style."

By the time Static flew into his bedroom window, it was getting late. He took off his mask, his long coat, and the black shirt with his gold Static logo on it. He looked in the mirror.

Virgil Hawkins stared back at him. Static was a

super hero, but Virgil was just an average teenager. A kid who had ten pages of homework to finish before school tomorrow. His geometry book was on his desk.

"Fighting Goopzilla was a lot easier than geometry," he moaned.

The next day at school, he told his best friend, Richie Foley, all about his scuffle with the thief and his fight with the germ creature. Richie was the only one who knew that Virgil and Static were the same person.

They whispered at a table in the back of their science lab. Richie was tinkering with a pair of miniature walkie-talkies. His spiky blond hair stuck up from the top of his head. He examined the wires through his black-rimmed glasses while listening to Virgil.

"Do you think it was a Bang Baby?" Richie asked.

Richie knew that Virgil had gotten his superpowers in a chemical explosion they called the Big Bang. A bunch of people got caught in the Big Bang and they all ended up with superpowers. People started calling them Bang Babies.

Virgil shook his head. "No way that thing was ever human! I just hope I zapped it for keeps."

Richie pointed to a wire on one of the walkie-talkies. "Speaking of zaps, could you give me a hand here?"

Virgil checked to make sure no one was looking, then pointed his finger at the wire. A little spark shot out and hit the tip, melting the metal. Now the wire was attached to the control panel.

Richie grinned. "Perfect-o," he said. "Just think, when we finish these, not only will we ace Science Lab, we'll have our own crime-stoppin' walkie-talkies."

Virgil smiled back. He didn't know what he'd do without Richie as a best friend. Richie helped Virgil figure out how to use his powers. He even helped make Virgil's costume and his metal flying disk. Richie was all about the gear. Without gear, being a super hero wasn't much fun.

Suddenly, the door to the science lab banged open. A tall, pretty girl with long, brown hair stomped through the lab. She slammed her books down on Virgil and Richie's table and sat down in an empty chair. She didn't say anything. She just sat there, looking angry.

"You okay, Frieda?" Virgil asked.

"No!" Frieda snapped. "Didn't you hear? The school board just cut the budget for the journalism club by forty percent. How are we supposed to put out a school newspaper without any money?"

Richie and Virgil shrugged.

"Yeah, and meanwhile, they haven't taken any money away from the sports teams," Frieda continued. "It's not fair! It's like they think football is more important than the news."

"I guess —" Virgil started, but Frieda was on a roll.

"And you know what really ticks me off? I wrote a great story about this, but they won't let me publish it in the newspaper," she fumed. "What ever happened to freedom of speech? We have to take action!"

Virgil couldn't help smiling. Frieda always took things so seriously.

"That's right, girl," he teased. "Power to the people!"

Richie grinned. "Yeah! We'll chain ourselves to our lockers!"

"We'll go on strike!" Virgil added.

Richie and Virgil pounded their fists on the table. "Strike! Strike! Strike!" Then they both burst out laughing.

Frieda thought they were serious. She jumped to her feet.

"Virgil, you're a genius!" she cried.

"I am?" Virgil asked.

Frieda didn't answer him. She ran out of the science lab.

Richie shrugged. He leaned over and put the finishing touch on the walkie-talkies.

"Let's test these babies out after school," Richie said. "I can't wait!"

After the last bell rang, Virgil and Richie met in the front hallway. Richie held the walkie-talkies.

"Just got to get my jacket," Richie said, but when they turned the corner, security tape blocked the hallway. Mr. Janus, the school janitor, was mopping the floor.

"'Scuze me," Richie said, crawling under the tape. "Can I just —"

"No, you cannot!" Mr. Janus snapped. "One of your grubby little classmates spilled juice on the floor. I have declared this entire area off-limits!"

Mr. Janus dipped his mop into a bucket of green liquid. Richie and Virgil backed away, holding their noses.

"That stuff reeks!" Richie cried.

"Kinda like my sister's cooking," Virgil joked.

Richie shrugged. "Guess I'll get my jacket tomorrow," he said. "Come on, let's test the walkie-talkies."

Virgil found a secluded spot, got suited up in his Static gear, and the boys headed downtown.

Richie stationed himself on the roof of an apartment building. Static flew between the buildings around him. He clipped the walkie-talkie to the collar of his jacket.

"Static to Richie. Static to Richie. Do you hear me, bro?" he called.

Richie spoke into his walkie-talkie. "Loud and clear! Told you they'd work!"

"What do we call these gizmos?" Static asked.

Richie thought for a minute. "How about Shock-Vox?"

Static nodded. "ShockVox. Yeah, I like it!"

Static zoomed between two narrow buildings. Then he swooped up and swirled around, making a figure eight in the air. Sometimes he thought flying on his disk was the best thing about being a super hero. He loved seeing Dakota City from up high. He could see everything. The high school, the park, the crowds of people screaming and running from the meatpacking plant . . .

Screaming and running? "Uh-oh," Static said. He flew toward the plant.

As he got closer, something rose up behind the building. A huge, slimy creature that looked like it was made of green goop.

"Richie! It's Goopzilla again!" Static said into the ShockVox.

Static swooped down. The creature had knocked over a meat delivery truck and was stuffing raw beef into its body. The meat dissolved inside the squishy green slime.

"Whoa! He's got the munchies!" Static exclaimed.

The creature reached into the truck to get more

meat. Static hurled a ball of lightning at the truck. The charge hit the creature, and it backed off.

Static flew down, hovering over the creature's head. "Better lay off the beef! It's gonna mess up your cholesterol!"

Static hurled ball after ball of lightning at Goopzilla. It ducked each blast. Then a mass of thick, fingerlike things shot out of the front of the creature! They wriggled like snakes.

One of the fingers reached out to grab Static. He did a wild loop-the-loop in the air to avoid it. The metal disk sliced through some of the slimy fingers. They went flying, and the creature let out an angry roar. It slammed Static's disk with its remaining fingers.

Static tumbled to the ground and landed with a thud next to the meat truck.

"Ow!" He turned to Goopzilla. "Hey, man! That was an accident — but this won't be!"

Static jumped to his feet. He used his power to lift the metal truck into the air. It floated up off the ground toward Goopzilla.

Then the weirdest thing happened. The truck

passed *right through the creature's body*, leaving a big hole, which closed back up instantly.

Still, the creature must have had enough. It sank back into the ground.

"That's right," Static said, exhausted. "You better run!"

Then Static noticed something. One of the creature's fingers was crawling away from him.

"Oh, no you don't," Static said. He jumped up on his flying disk. He zipped up to a streetlight and zapped off the glass light globe and the metal plate that went with it, then zoomed back down.

Whomp! He slammed the heavy glass globe down on the squirming finger, then slid the metal plate underneath.

"Here's the scoop, Mister Goop," Static declared, grinning. "You are mine!"

CHAPTER THREE
Get It Off Me!

"Richie! Meet me in the park right away! I've got something you gotta see!" Virgil whispered into his ShockVox.

Virgil put the glass globe in his backpack. He headed to the park and waited for Richie. His friend showed up a few minutes later.

"This better be good," Richie said, panting. "I had to run ten blocks."

Virgil opened his backpack. "Peep this, Rich."

The green slimy finger wriggled around inside the glass.

Richie's eyes widened. "What *is* that thing?"

"It's a little piece of Goopzilla," Virgil said. "I figure we can stay after Science Lab tomorrow and take a closer look at it."

"Why not now?" Richie asked.

Virgil shook his head. "School's closed, Rich."

Richie shrugged. "Your point?"

"Uh, a little something called breaking and entering," Virgil reminded him.

"V, there's a giant meat-eating creature roaming around Dakota City," Richie said. "We gotta figure out what it's made of before it eats the whole town!"

Richie had a point. They left the park and hopped on a city bus, not realizing that behind them, the creature rose up from the park lawn. It knew Virgil had its missing finger. And it wanted it back.

It was getting dark when Virgil and Richie got to the school. Outside on the field, the school marching band was practicing. Nobody noticed Virgil and Richie sneak up to the side door. They slipped into the school without a problem.

The boys turned down the hall and headed

toward the science lab. Virgil sniffed the air. Something smelled strange.

"Do you smell something?" he asked Richie.

"Sorry," Richie said. "I had the chili fries for lunch."

"No," Virgil said. "It almost smells like —"

Suddenly, the boys bumped right into the school janitor!

"Mr. Janus!" Virgil cried.

The janitor was mopping the floor with the smelly cleaner. He scowled at the boys.

"What in blue blazes are you doing here?" he asked. "Don't you know the school's closed?"

Virgil looked at Richie. They hadn't come up with a plan in case they were caught.

Richie thought fast. "Uh, we never left! We stayed so late because geometry class was so interesting . . ."

". . . we thought there might be another one!" Virgil finished.

"Bye!" Richie said quickly.

The boys turned around and raced away.

"No running!" Mr. Janus shouted after them. "I've got wet floors all over the place!"

The boys turned down another hallway. This time, they bumped into somebody else — Frieda!

"What are you doing here?" Virgil and Frieda said at once.

"I, uh, asked you first," Virgil said.

Three more students walked around the corner. Kim, a girl with spiky black hair and glasses, Leon, a tall, skinny kid, and Omar, a big, round kid with dark hair. They were all on the newspaper staff with Frieda.

"It was Frieda's idea," Kim said.

"She taped the door," Leon added.

"We are totally innocent!" Omar said. They all looked nervous.

Frieda gave them a warning look. "Sshhh, you guys!"

They were up to something. Then again, he and Richie were up to something, too. Virgil suddenly remembered the creepy-crawly thing in his backpack.

"Uh, we were never here," Virgil said, backing away.

"Neither were we!" said Frieda.

Virgil and Richie went to the science lab and

quietly closed the door behind them. Richie took the cover off a large microscope. Then he got two plastic face masks and handed one to Virgil.

"Can't be too careful," he said. Virgil nodded. They put on plastic gloves as well.

Virgil took the heavy glass globe out of his backpack. The Goopzilla finger wriggled inside. Richie picked up a pair of tongs.

"Show me the patient," he said.

Virgil slowly lifted up the globe.

"Easy . . . easy," Richie said.

Virgil opened the lid a little higher.

In a flash, the slimy finger jumped out of the globe.

Splat! It landed on Richie's face mask. Green slime oozed from it as it stuck to the plastic.

"Aaaaahhh!" Richie cried. "Get it off me!"

"Hold still, Richie!" Virgil said.

Virgil carefully slapped his hands on both sides of the face mask, giving the creature a quick zap. Richie's hair stood straight up from the charge.

The finger let go of its grasp, and Virgil peeled it off.

"I got it!" Virgil cried.

But the creature wasn't done yet. With another splat, it jumped onto *Virgil's* face mask.

"It's got me!" Virgil yelled.

Keep cool, he told himself. *You can handle this thing.*

Virgil zapped the slimy finger again. It slid off, and he slapped it down on one of the tables. He grabbed the glass globe and slammed it down on top of the finger. Then he put a heavy encyclopedia on top of the thick glass.

Richie was still shaking. He grabbed a pair of tweezers.

"Don't move," he told Virgil.

Richie reached up and pulled a little piece of the green finger out of Virgil's hair. It looked like a slimy little worm.

"Now, that's disgusting," Virgil said, making a face.

"But useful," Richie said. He brought the little piece to the microscope and put it on a slide. Then he slipped the slide under the microscope. Richie looked through one of the lenses while Virgil looked through the other.

Richie let out a low whistle. "That's weird. Most of the cells here look like normal dirt. But what are those glowing purple ones?"

Virgil looked up from the lens. "They're the same color as the Big Bang gas," he realized. "This creature must be a Bang Baby after all!"

"You're kidding," Richie said.

Virgil thought about it. "The chemical from the Big Bang must have seeped into the ground," he guessed, "turning the bacteria and stuff there into meta-microbes!"

Richie nodded. "At least we know what it is now. But there's still one problem."

"What's that?" Virgil asked.

Richie frowned. "How are we supposed to stop the biggest Bang Baby ever made?"

CHAPTER FOUR
On the Loose

While Virgil and Richie were busy trying to figure out exactly what Goopzilla was, Frieda and her friends were busy in the newspaper office.

Frieda held up the front page of a newspaper before the others.

"If the school won't let us protest the cuts for the journalism department, we'll do it ourselves," Frieda said. "This tells the whole story. Now all we have to do is sign it."

She held out a pen. Leon, Kim, and Omar looked at each other nervously.

"Do it for freedom of speech!" Frieda urged.

Omar took the pen, but before he could sign, they heard a noise. Frieda looked at the glass window on the classroom door. A shadow passed by it.

"Mr. Janus is coming!" Frieda said. "Everybody hide!"

Kim dove behind a printer. Omar and Leon crawled behind the teacher's desk. Frieda turned off the lights and crouched beside the door.

Mr. Janus peered through the window. He frowned, but moved on without opening the door. Frieda and the others heard a click.

"Don't tell me he locked the door," Leon said when Mr. Janus was safely gone.

All four students ran to the door. Omar pulled on the knob.

"Okay, I won't tell you," Omar said.

"That's just great," Frieda moaned.

Back in the science lab, Virgil and Richie were having a problem of their own.

Still looking at the little piece of Goopzilla under the microscope, they heard a loud thump and a crash.

They whirled around. The rest of the Goopzilla finger had knocked over the glass globe — and

escaped! Virgil and Richie looked around franti-
cally. Virgil spotted the finger.

"There!" he cried. The slimy finger was plas-
tered against the window.

Zap! Virgil lobbed a lightning bolt at it. It
jumped off the window onto the wall, where it began to slither up.

Virgil shot another bolt at it, but missed. The
finger slid into a wall vent — and disappeared.

"I gotta get it," Virgil said. He climbed up on a
table. The vent led to a narrow air shaft. He pulled
himself into the shaft.

Richie handed Virgil a ShockVox. "Happy
crawling!" he said.

The air shaft was a tight squeeze. Virgil had to
crawl through it on his belly.

"Here, goopy, goopy!" he called out. He wanted
to find that thing — fast.

Virgil shot out a small spark with his fingers.
They lit up the dark shaft for a second. He saw the
slimy green finger heading for a T-shaped break
in the path. There were two ways to turn — left or
right.

Which way had the finger gone? Virgil wasn't sure.

He sighed. "Great. Big-time super hero chases runaway sausage," he cracked.

Virgil turned right — right into a cluster of cockroaches!

The shiny brown insects skittered all over him. His skin crawled as he felt their tiny legs pass over him.

"Get off! Get off!" he cried. He squirmed around, trying to brush them away.

Virgil couldn't see where he was going. He tumbled into another air shaft, and slid all the way down it, landing at the bottom with a thud.

"This just isn't my day," Virgil sighed.

Back in the science lab, Richie waited to hear from Virgil. He looked out the window.

The band members were marching up and down the field, playing the same song over and over. Richie yawned.

Then something rose up from behind the bleachers. Something big and slimy and green!

"Goopzilla!" Richie cried. He had never seen it before.

The creature chased after band members. It slurped a tuba right out of a player's arms. The tuba player ran off, screaming. Goopzilla absorbed the tuba into its gooey body, then spat it right back out.

"Guess it's still hungry!" Richie switched on the ShockVox.

"Virgil? Are you there?" he called. "We've got a little problem out here!"

CHAPTER FIVE
The Chase

"Goopzilla's on the field," Richie told Virgil. "And it thinks the marching band is a major snack!"

"I'm on it!" Virgil replied.

The missing finger would have to wait. Virgil looked around for a way to exit the shaft. He saw a vent beneath him.

Virgil zapped the cover off the shaft and jumped down — right into the classroom below.

Frieda and her crew were standing by the classroom door. Frieda was trying to pick the lock with a bent paper clip. They were shocked to see Virgil.

"Virgil? What are you doing here?" Frieda demanded.

Oh no, Virgil thought. *More excuses.*

"Well, there was this frog in biology class, see?" Virgil lied. "It hopped into the air shaft, and I went after it. That's when I, uh, dropped in."

Virgil clapped his hands. "Well, gotta go."

"The door's locked," Frieda said. "It won't budge."

"Oh, boy," Virgil groaned. "Not good. Not good."

Frieda and her friends began to argue about the best way to open the door. Virgil stepped to the side and whispered into the ShockVox. He explained the situation to Richie.

"I can't power up to open the door," Virgil said. "If they see me, I'm busted!"

Richie's voice came through the ShockVox. "I got an idea, V. Sit tight!"

Richie raced down the hallway. All he needed was a key to the door of the journalism room. Mr. Janus had keys to every room in the school. He hoped Mr. Janus would be too busy cleaning to notice Richie swiping the keys.

Richie tiptoed down the hallway and turned a corner. Mr. Janus had his back to Richie, mopping the floor. The keys stuck out of his back pocket. Richie reached out to grab them. . . .

Whack! Mr. Janus threw his mop over his shoulder, accidentally hitting Richie in the face! Richie flew back with a thud.

Mr. Janus spun around, angry.

"You're in trouble now!" he cried.

Then the angry look on Mr. Janus's face morphed into one of shock. He stared up at the wall. So did Richie.

Goopzilla's finger slithered on the wall above the lockers.

"What in the name of Mr. Clean is that?" Mr. Janus wondered. He grabbed his mop. "I just cleaned there, you grimy glob!"

As Mr. Janus chased after the runaway finger, Richie grabbed the keys.

"Success!" Richie cried. He ran down the hallway, heading straight for the journalism room.

"I'll get you out," Richie called through the window. He stuck the key in the lock.

It wouldn't budge. The lock was jammed.

"Because of Frieda's paper clip!" Kim said.

Virgil couldn't wait any longer. He pushed his way through the others. Then he covered the doorknob with his hands, making sure to hide his electro-powers.

"Richie, try one more time," he said, hoping his friend would get the hint. "Turn it hard. I'll pull!"

Richie nodded. So that the others wouldn't realize what he was doing, Virgil carefully aimed a small magnetic field at the paper clip inside the doorknob. It came loose, and the door opened.

"All right!" Leon cheered. "We're out of here!"

They all stepped out into the hallway. Only Frieda held back.

"But we've all got to sign the newspaper in protest," she reminded them. "We've got to do it for —"

Frieda didn't finish. The giant Goopzilla had become bored with the marching band and was sliding down the hallway, heading right for them!

"Everybody chill," Virgil said calmly. "Don't let it know you're afraid."

Only Richie listened. Frieda, Leon, Kim, and Omar turned around and tore down the hallway, screaming. Goopzilla sped down the hallway after them, roaring.

"Maybe they have the right idea," Richie said.

Virgil nodded, and they both ran. The hallway divided into three directions. Omar kept running straight. Frieda ran left. Leon and Kim ran right. Virgil and Richie followed Leon and Kim.

The creature stopped. The slime inside its body gurgled and snarled.

Then Goopzilla split into three different pieces! One piece went straight, one went left, and the last went right. No one was safe!

Virgil saw Leon and Kim bolt into the cafeteria. He and Richie darted into an empty classroom.

"Better get in gear, V," Richie said.

Virgil nodded. In a flash, he changed into his Static gear. Then he hopped on his flying disk and flew out into the hall just in time to see a big piece of Goopzilla ooze into the cafeteria. Static flew after it.

Leon and Kim were screaming in terror as

Goopzilla roared over them, waving its stringy arms.

Static zapped a nearby vending machine and sent it flying toward Goopzilla.

"Snack on that!" Static cried.

CHAPTER SIX
Clean-Up Time

The machine slammed into the creature, sending it squishing against a wall — but it wouldn't be down for long. Static quickly energized two metal chairs. They flew underneath Leon and Kim and swept them off their feet.

"School's out, folks!" Static said.

He made the chairs fly out the window and watched them land safely on the ground below.

Then Static heard a noise behind him. He turned to see the piece of Goopzilla shaking the snack machine upside down. The bags of junk food fell into its gooey body and were absorbed by its slimy green flesh.

Static shook his head. His electric bolts didn't seem to harm Goopzilla at all. "When they say germs are harder to kill these days, they're not kidding!" he moaned.

Then Static heard another sound — a cry for help. He zoomed back into the hallway. Another piece of Goopzilla was chasing Omar down the hall.

Static flew toward Omar as the boy rounded a corner.

Splat! The floor was wet from Mr. Janus's mopping. Omar slid and landed on his back.

Static flew up behind him and helped him back on his feet.

"How can there be two of them?" Static wondered. He hadn't seen Goopzilla split into three parts.

The creature roared as it chased after them, but when it came to the puddle on the floor, it stopped.

"That's weird," Static said. But it was a good thing, too. It gave them time to get away. Static pulled Omar onto his flying disk and zipped through the window, leaving Omar outside with Leon and Kim.

Static flew back inside. There were at least two hungry Goopzillas squishing around in there. And Frieda and Richie were still inside. He had to find the Goopzillas and stop them! Static thought he knew what to do.

He heard Frieda crying for help. He flew toward the sound. On the way, he found Mr. Janus's janitor's bucket. He grabbed the mop and held it like a sword. He used his power to move the metal bucket alongside his disk.

The sound was coming from the girls' room. Static burst through the doors, holding the mop in front of him. Stinky floor cleaner dripped from the mop head.

Frieda was backed into a corner. Goopzilla — or one of the Goopzillas — was towering over her, making hungry noises!

"En garde!" Static shouted. He thrust the mop into Goopzilla's squishy body. The creature let out a horrible shriek.

Static kept pummeling the creature with the

mop. Finally, he kicked over the janitor's bucket. The floor cleaner splashed toward Goopzilla.

But the creature was quick. It jumped up, sticking to the ceiling. Static quickly grabbed Frieda and flew out of the room.

They made it all the way down the hallway when they heard a noise. Goopzilla burst out of the girls' room. Then another Goopzilla slithered down the hall toward it. And a third Goopzilla slithered in from another direction.

Static watched as the three creatures melded together to make one whole Goopzilla again.

"It must have split itself up to go after us," Static realized.

The creature slid down the hallway, away from them.

"It's running away!" Frieda cried.

"No, just looking for more food. And the whole city's on its menu!" Static said.

"What are you going to do?" Frieda asked.

Static smiled. "Spoil its appetite."

Static flew off on his disk until he found the closet where Mr. Janus kept his supplies. He zapped open the door and found just what he needed — two giant drums of floor cleaner. The label read KILLS GERMS DEAD!

Static zapped the drums and they rose into the air. He kept them suspended and went flying toward the angry sound of Goopzilla.

Static found the creature in the school parking lot.

"Yo, Goopy!" Static called out.

The creature stopped and turned around.

"You still got the munchies?" Static asked. He waved to the creature. "Well, here I am! Come get your grub on!"

It worked. Goopzilla charged across the parking lot at superspeed, but Static was ready for him.

Static sent the metal drums of cleaner flying up, up, and over Goopzilla. Then he blasted both drums with lightning bolts.

They exploded and smelly green cleaner splashed all over the giant germ. It screamed and waved its arms, and then dissolved. It just fizzled out. Seconds later, all that was left was a harmless puddle of goo.

"Mmm," Static quipped. "Lemon-fresh scent, too!"

Static changed out of his gear just as the police and news crews arrived. He met up with Richie. Frieda and the other kids from the newspaper ran up to the reporters.

"Why were you in the school after it was closed?" a reporter asked.

"We were staging a protest," Frieda said. "The school has cut the budget for the journalism department. We don't think it's fair, so we published a special edition of the newspaper on the subject."

Virgil smiled. This was just the break Frieda needed. The school would have to listen to her now.

"Man, they're getting all the attention," Richie complained. "Don't you want to be interviewed, too?"

Virgil shrugged. "I've got nothing to say," he said. Then he grinned. "Besides — I feel like I just caught a germ!"

CHAPTER SEVEN
Little Johnny Morrow

Virgil felt pretty good about taking care of Goopzilla. That weekend he decided to take a break. He hung out at the Dakota Mall with Richie and their friend Daisy, a pretty girl with short, dark hair.

The friends grabbed lunch at the food court and found a table next to a railing, which overlooked all the stores on the first floor.

"Great mall, huh?" Daisy remarked.

"It's okay," Virgil replied, shrugging. "It's no Kid Circus, though."

"Kid Circus?" Daisy asked.

Richie slurped his soda. "An amusement park we went to when we were kids. They shut it down years ago, but there's still a little bit left of it behind the mall."

Daisy frowned. "Oh, that's sad. It's like they paved over a piece of your childhood."

"Yeah, it's tragic," Virgil joked. He and Richie leaned into each other, pretending to sob. Then they started to crack up.

Daisy shook her head. "Don't you two take anything seriously?"

They were about to.

While Virgil and his friends were goofing around in the food court, something more serious was happening in a jewelry store down below.

A young man dressed in a purple shirt with a big pink stripe walked up to the case of men's watches. A salesman in a fancy suit approached him.

"May I help you, sir?" the salesman sniffed.

"Tell me about that one," the man said, pointing to an expensive-looking watch in the case.

"Ah, yes," said the salesman. "That's the Chrono-tech 2000. It's a timepiece, a pager, and a wireless Internet browser all in one."

The salesman took the watch out of the case. He started to hand it to the man in purple, but stopped. "Excuse me, but you look familiar. Do I know you?"

"Well, duh," said the man. "I'm Johnny Morrow."

"Who?" the salesman asked.

Johnny scowled. "Little Johnny Morrow. I was ten years old and I had my own TV series — *Johnny on the Spot!*" He got a faraway look in his eyes. "My face was on T-shirts and lunch boxes. The whole country loved me. They wanted to talk like me, dress like me, and be — me. But then the network dumped me and it all stopped. The fans, the money — all gone!"

The salesman snatched away the watch. "I see. Well, have a good day."

Johnny held out his arm. "What are you doing?"

"Well, you just said you don't have any money," the salesman stammered.

Johnny raised an eyebrow. "Who needs money? You're going to give it to me."

"Says who?" demanded the salesman.

Johnny Morrow grinned. He pointed to either side of the salesman.

"Says them!" he cried.

In an instant, two more men who looked just like Johnny Morrow appeared next to the salesman. He gasped.

The two Johnny clones reached into the watch case and grabbed handfuls of watches. They handed some to the real Johnny. The salesman recovered just in time to press the alarm button under the counter.

The sound of the ringing alarm blared through the mall, but Johnny had what he wanted. He and his clones ran out of the jewelry store.

Up in the food court, Virgil jumped when he heard the alarm. He, Richie, and Daisy looked down over the railing. They saw Johnny running out of the store, his hands full of watches.

"It's a robbery!" Virgil cried.

Then the two Johnny clones followed, carrying more watches.

"Make that robber*ies,* bro," Richie corrected. "Check it out. They're like triplets or something."

Johnny and his clones began ransacking the mall. Virgil watched as one of them went into a stereo store and came back out rolling a giant TV.

Virgil had to stop them, but Daisy was right there. She knew nothing about his Static identity.

"I gotta jet," he whispered to Richie. "Any ideas?"

"Think food poisoning," Richie replied.

Virgil got the hint. He doubled over, grabbing his stomach.

"Olllph!" he moaned.

"Virgil! What's wrong?" Daisy asked.

Virgil covered his mouth with his hands.

"Are you sick, V?" Richie asked.

Virgil nodded.

"There's a restroom on the other side of the food court," Daisy said.

Virgil nodded again and staggered off toward the restroom. Once he got there, he quickly changed into his super hero gear.

Static flew through the food court on his metal disk, and down to the floor below. Johnny and his clones, surrounded by their loot, were giving each other high fives.

Static hovered over them, grinning.

"You know what they say," he said. "The family that does crime together, does *time* together!"

CHAPTER EIGHT
Replay

"Yo! Static!"

The shoppers in the mall clapped and cheered when Static appeared.

Johnny Morrow and his clones frowned. "Well, listen to that! The hero has fans," Johnny said bitterly. "But take my word for it, Static. They'll turn on you. They always do."

Static floated down closer to the three Johnnys.

"Thanks for the advice," he said. "Now, are you boys going to come quietly?"

"Why?" Johnny asked. "You're outnumbered."

Static shrugged. "Three to one? I've faced more than that."

"Let's count, shall we?" said Johnny. "One, two, three . . ."

Then Johnny pointed three more times. "Four! Five! Six!" Each time he pointed, a new replica appeared.

"I've heard of triplets," Virgil said. "What are you guys? Six-lets?"

The new clones popped up in front of a golf store. They each grabbed a club, swung, and sent a ball shooting through the air at Static.

Static rode his flying disk like a skateboard, ducking each golf ball as it whizzed past him.

"Ha! Missed me!" Static cried.

But three more balls zoomed at him, knocking into his legs. Static tumbled off his disk onto the floor. Immediately, all six Johnnys jumped on him.

Static struggled, but they were too much for him. Two of the look-alikes dragged him to his feet. Across the room, the other four picked up an iron bench. They charged toward him, ready to ram him with it.

But Static's hands were free. He pointed his fingers at the bench, zapping it with an electric charge. The bench flew back against the wall, pinning the four clones there.

The two Johnny clones holding Static let out an angry growl. They dragged him up to the food court, then hurled him over the railing!

Static thought fast. Strings of tiny white lights hung across the ceiling above them. He quickly zapped them, and the strands fell down into his hands. Static swung like Tarzan across the mall. He flew through the window of a hat store and landed safely in a pile of hats. A cowboy hat and a hat with a pink feather landed on his head. He shook them off.

"None of these match my gear!" he joked.

Static got to his feet. He could see the six look-alikes running through the mall. He ran out of the store and found his metal disk on the floor. He hopped on. "Let's see where these bad boys are headed."

Static spotted a clone in a purple shirt running through the parking lot. He followed him to the back of the mall. The Johnny clone hopped over a chain-link fence. A rusted sign warned, DEMOLITION SITE. DO NOT ENTER!

Static recognized the crumbling buildings behind the fence. It was the old site of Kid Circus. A strange place for a hideout.

"Well, at least I know my way around," he reasoned.

The clone didn't seem to know he was being followed, so Static decided to play it sneaky. He followed him into an abandoned building, staying hidden in the shadows.

One of the guys in purple was talking to the other five clones. They were in the old hall of mirrors, Static realized. Narrow hallways made up a maze of mirror-covered walls, making it tricky to find the way out. Most of the mirrors were broken and cracked.

"Did Static follow you or not?" Johnny was asking one of the clones.

The clone shrugged. "Dunno."

Johnny scowled. "You know what? You make me embarrassed to be me. In fact — get out of my sight!"

Johnny pointed at the replica, who vanished in a blink.

Static was horrified. He jumped out of his hiding place.

"What is with you, man? You just wiped out your own brother!" Static cried.

Johnny shook his head. "My what? You've got it wrong."

Johnny snapped his fingers. The other four clones blinked away, too.

"They're duplicates," Johnny said proudly. "Energy clones. Made them all by myself."

Static finally got it. "You're a meta-human," he said.

"Duh," Johnny said sarcastically.

Static realized something else, too. "Don't I know you from somewhere?"

"Well, I did have my own TV show when I was ten," Johnny boasted.

"Oh, yeah," Static said. "What's-his-name."

Johnny looked angry. "Johnny Morrow!" He was steaming. "But you can call me Replay!"

Replay clenched his fists, and immediately five more clones blinked to life. They surrounded Static.

Static frowned. To capture Replay for good, he'd have to get the *real* one — not one of the energy clones. But now he couldn't tell which one was real!

One of the Replays charged at Static with a kung fu kick. Static blocked the kick with his arms, but the blow sent him staggering back into two more clones. They tripped him, sending him thudding into one of the mirrors.

Static stared at his reflection. "Well? Any ideas?"

The mirror cracked. But at that moment, Static remembered something. He smiled, then got to his feet and turned to the Replays.

"You know, when I was a kid, I spent a lot of time bumping around the hall of mirrors," Static said.

"So?" the Replays said.

"So, I finally figured out that the trick was not to

look in front of you . . . but to follow the footprints on the floor!"

Static dropped to one knee. He slapped his palms on the floor, then sent out a static charge.

Static knew the charge wouldn't affect the energy clones, just the real Replay.

He was right. One of the Replays jumped up, shocked by the charge. Static moved quickly. He shoved the real Replay against a wall.

"I'm going to make so many of me, you won't have a prayer!" Replay snarled.

"Ooh, a room full of has-beens," Static taunted. "Now I *am* scared."

Replay pushed Static away. Static made a fist and started building up an electric charge. Replay tensed.

Static punched with his fist, aiming a huge electric blast at Replay. At the same exact moment, Replay let loose a burst of cloning energy.

Wham! The two superpowered energy fields slammed together. The hall of mirrors shook, rocked by the explosion. Static went flying back into a bank of mirrors. Then everything went black.

When he opened his eyes, he saw his own face staring back at him! Static rose to his feet.

An exact duplicate of him was standing there.

Static blinked. "What the — "

Then, suddenly, the hall of mirrors began to shake. Static looked up. A support beam cracked and came tumbling down.

Static moved to escape, but was too late. The beam came crashing down on him.

Static groaned as everything went black once more.

CHAPTER NINE
Bad Static!

Static slowly woke up. He remembered the beam falling down, and he remembered seeing himself — doubled! He jumped to his feet.

But the other Static wasn't there. Static looked around at all of the mirrors.

"Must have been a reflection," Static said. "Yeah, that's all. A reflection."

He was wrong. Somehow, a Static clone had been created during the blast. And while the real Static was trapped in the hall of mirrors, his double was busy at the mall.

Back at the mall, Richie and Daisy were looking

for Virgil. They went outside when they heard the sound of police sirens.

They looked toward the sound. Down the street, Static was swooping down from the sky. At least, it looked like Static. They didn't know it, but it was really Static's clone!

"It's Static!" Richie said. He felt relieved. He had been hoping nothing bad had happened to Virgil.

"Maybe Static caught those look-alike guys," Daisy said.

Richie and Daisy ran toward Static. Then they stopped, shocked.

The Static clone was zapping the ATMs at a bank. With each zap, money flew out of the ATMs. Static swooped down and scooped up the cash, stuffing it into a plastic trash bag.

Richie couldn't believe it. What was his friend doing? He ran up to him.

"Have you lost your mind?" Richie demanded.

The Static clone looked up. It pointed at Richie, making him float in the air. Richie floated higher and higher until, *wham!* He landed on a billboard, stuck there by static electricity. A bunch of police officers were stuck up there, too.

"How could you do this to me?" Richie called down.

The crowd began to boo and hiss at the Static clone. He just ignored it. He flew away from the bank and landed on the rooftop of an office building. Replay and his clones were waiting for him.

Replay took the bags of cash from the Static clone. Then he leaned over the building. He smiled when he heard the angry crowd.

"Your fans don't look too happy, Static," Replay said. "Well, like we say in the biz, they ain't seen nothin' yet!"

Meanwhile, Virgil had no idea the Static clone was up to no good. He stumbled home, his head still hurting from the fallen beam. When he got there, his sister, Sharon, and their dad had already started dinner. Sharon had set out a plate for him.

Sharon heard him come through the door. "Well, if you like to eat your dinner cold, it's fine with —" she started. Then she saw her brother's dirt-streaked face. "Hey, you look like you were hit with a ton of bricks!"

"Try a ton and a half," Virgil groaned, sinking into his seat.

"You're not the only one," said Mr. Hawkins. "The whole city's in an uproar."

"About what?" Virgil asked. He stuffed a forkful of mashed potatoes into his mouth.

"About Static turning outlaw," Sharon said.

Virgil nearly choked on his potatoes. "Say what?"

Sharon picked up a TV remote, aimed it at a small TV on the kitchen counter, and flicked on the screen.

Virgil watched, shocked. The news showed somebody who looked just like Static robbing the ATMs.

The news reporter looked sad. "All of Dakota City is in shock," she said. "The hero we all admired has disappointed us."

Sharon shook her head and turned off the TV.

Virgil felt like he was in some kind of nightmare. "This can't be happening!" he said.

CHAPTER TEN
It Wasn't Me!

Virgil could barely finish his dinner. Something must have happened when his electric blast collided with Replay's energy burst. A Static clone had been created. And now it was giving Static a bad name all over Dakota City.

Virgil had to stop it — fast. And there was only one person who could help him — Richie.

After supper, Virgil ran up to his room and gave him a call. No answer. Virgil tried again. And again. That was weird. Richie always picked up for Virgil.

"Maybe his phone's not working," Virgil guessed.

So he headed over to Richie's and knocked on the front door.

Richie opened the door a tiny crack.

"Go away!" he hissed.

"Come on, Rich, it's important," Virgil pleaded. "Let me in!"

"No, thanks," Richie said. "I don't want to spend the rest of the night stuck to my ceiling."

Virgil shook his head. "You don't really think I did that to you, do you? I can explain."

Richie frowned. "I don't know. All of the other meta-humans are criminals. Maybe it just took you longer to go wacko. Maybe you have a split personality!"

"Close," Virgil said. "It happened in the hall of mirrors. I chased Replay there, right? We fought. There was this big explosion. When I woke up, I saw someone who looked just like me. I think Replay cloned me!"

Richie looked sad. "That's your explanation? You definitely *have* gone wacko," he said.

Richie closed the door and locked it. Virgil felt lower than low. Even his best friend thought he had gone bad!

The next morning, Virgil sulked around the house. He and Richie usually figured things out together. Without his friend, he wasn't sure what to do. Virgil went downtown and walked around, trying to clear his head. He smelled something delicious.

Virgil looked up. He had walked all the way to the Get Your Grub On café, his favorite place to chow down.

"Maybe some soul food will cheer me up," Virgil said hopefully. He went inside and found a small table in the corner.

But the café had a TV on, tuned in to the news. The police were giving a news conference. Virgil recognized Chief Barnstable. Usually, the police chief was happy to get Static's help.

"Today the police department has formed the Dakota Meta-Human Capture Division," he said. "This new group will have weapons that will capture, but not harm, meta-humans. Any questions?"

A reporter raised her hand. "Chief Barnstable, what about Static?" she asked.

Chief Barnstable looked sad. "Static has

changed," he said. "From now on, we will treat him just like any other meta-human."

The picture on the screen changed suddenly. A reporter was talking quickly into the microphone.

"Breaking news!" she said. "Static has struck again!"

"No, he *hasn't*!" Virgil said out loud. The other customers looked at him strangely.

Virgil saw that it was true. The TV camera showed a jewelry store. Customers ran out screaming. Behind them flew the Static clone, carrying trays of jewelry under each arm.

Virgil's gloomy mood disappeared. He jumped out of his seat. "Okay, *now* I'm ticked!" he cried.

Virgil ran into the café's restroom. He flew out of the back door seconds later in his Static gear. Then he zoomed to the jewelry store. If he hurried, he could catch his clone.

But when Static got there, the look-alike was gone. People on the street shrieked and pointed when they saw him.

A tomato went flying past Static's face. Then an egg. The angry crowd was pelting him with food!

"It wasn't me!" Static shouted.

The crowd didn't believe him. Static flew away, dodging the flying food.

He didn't get far. A small army of police cars skidded to a stop below him. Chief Barnstable got out and put a bullhorn to his mouth. Three police officers ran up behind him. They each carried what looked like large tubes.

Static stopped in midair. Running from the police wasn't cool.

"Static, you are under arrest!" the chief shouted through the bullhorn.

"Chief, you can take me in, but you've got the wrong guy!" Static protested.

The chief frowned. "There's only one Static we know about," he shouted. "And you're him!"

Static had to make the chief believe him. "But —"

He didn't get a chance to finish. The three police officers aimed the tubes right at Static. A second later, three gas canisters came shooting out.

"Nooooo!" Static yelled.

CHAPTER ELEVEN
Replay's Next Move

Static waved his arms and surrounded himself with a ball of energy. The gas canisters hit the ball and bounced off.

Then two more officers ran up underneath Static. They shot a huge net out of another tube. Static flipped in the air, avoiding the net.

"Hey, that's not standard police gear!" Static cried.

The sound of a helicopter overhead drowned him out. Static looked down at the street below. There was a manhole right beneath him. An idea started to form.

"If I can't go up," he said, "I guess I'm going down!"

Static zapped the manhole cover and it flew off. Then he zoomed down into the sewer and the manhole cover slammed back down. It was so charged with electricity that no one would be able to remove it for a while. He'd have time to get away.

Static surfed through the sewers on his disk. He wrinkled his nose.

"Phew! I am definitely going to need a shower after *this*," he remarked.

Across town, Replay watched the whole scene on the news. He laughed.

"Yeah!" he cheered. He turned to Static's clone. "How about that, Static? Not much fun now that nobody loves you, right?"

The Static clone didn't reply.

Replay was about to look away when he noticed something on the Static Clone's collar — the ShockVox.

"Wonder what this is for," Replay said. He unclipped it and pressed a button on the ShockVox.

After Static escaped down the sewers, he came back out on the edge of Dakota City. He sat on top of a tall hill and just stared at the buildings. Things looked pretty grim. What was he going to do now?

Then he heard his ShockVox buzz. Had Richie changed his mind?

"Rich?" he answered.

Replay's voice came over the ShockVox instead. "No, not rich yet. But I'm working on it!"

"Replay!" Static cried. "Quit shredding my rep with that fake Static!"

Replay laughed. "Just stay tuned, buddy. Wait until you see what he does in the sequel."

Static rose to his feet. He had to stay calm. If Replay was planning something, he had to find out what it was. He had to stop it.

"What's left to steal?" Static asked. "You guys have pretty much ripped off everything of value in the city."

"Oh, Static, this next deal isn't about money," Replay said. "This time, it's personal!"

Then Replay disconnected.

"Wait!" Static cried angrily. He needed more information.

He looked at the ShockVox in his hand. It gave

him an idea. He needed Richie's help for it to work, though. Static flew to Richie's house, right through his bedroom window. Richie yelled when he saw Static.

"Shhh," Static said. "What are you afraid of?"

"You!" Richie said. "You're straight-up trippin' out!"

Static knew this wouldn't be easy. "You've got to help me, Richie. I need to prove I'm telling the truth. I need a favor."

Richie looked suspicious. "What favor?"

Static held out the ShockVox. "Can you rewire this thing to listen to another one? You know, like an intercom?"

"Who's got a ShockVox besides you and me?" Richie asked.

"The, uh, other me," Static said. "My evil twin."

Richie made a face — the face that said that Static had lost his mind. Static sighed. There was only one thing to do.

"Hey, if I really have turned bad, you don't have much of a choice, do you?" Static asked.

Richie got the point. He took the ShockVox from Static. He brought it to his desk and started messing with it. Soon a faint static noise came through the ShockVox.

"It should be working, but all I'm getting is noise," Richie said.

Static took the ShockVox from him. "Let me try," he said. He zapped the ShockVox with some extra energy.

Replay's voice came through loud and clear.

"So now you know my plan, boys," Replay was saying. "This time, it's about revenge!"

CHAPTER TWELVE
Canceled!

"Those idiots ruined my life, and now I'm going to ruin theirs," Replay continued. "You all know what to do, so let's do it!"

Replay's voice faded. Static turned to Richie.

"He talked about revenge," Static said. "What's the worst thing you can do to an actor?"

"Give them a bad review?" Richie guessed.

"No," Static said thoughtfully. "Fire them!"

Static ran to Richie's computer and pulled up a TV trivia Web site. He typed in Little Johnny Morrow and found what he was looking for.

"Aha!" Static said. "Little Johnny Morrow, star of *Johnny on the Spot*, got fired after four seasons on the DKT Network. Didn't they just build a new studio?"

"Yeah," Richie said, "the place downtown with the fountains and the outdoor TV."

Static jumped to his feet. "You coming?"

Richie didn't answer.

"Fine," he said. "Gotta fly!"

Static zoomed downtown to the DKT building. A huge TV screen in the front of the building was on. It showed a live game show that was being filmed inside.

Then Static spotted a shattered glass wall.

He was right. Replay *was* here, wreaking havoc. He just hoped he wasn't too late.

Static flew through the window and found a security guard sitting at his station, slumped over his seat. Static tried to wake him up.

"Who did this to you?" he asked.

The guard eyed him groggily. "You," he groaned, then fainted again.

"Figured you'd say that," Static said. He looked

at the security monitors. One of the screens showed Replay and his clones walking down a hallway on the fifth floor. Static took off for the nearest elevator.

When the elevator doors opened, Static heard a loud crash coming from down the hall. He followed the noise to a TV studio soundstage and flew inside.

Static recognized the set. It was the living room from the show *Finklestein's Monster*. Or at least, it was a living room.

Replay and the clones had trashed it, and they were just getting started. Replay lifted up a stage light and moved to hurl it against a wall.

Static shot a magnetic beam at the light, sending the light — and Replay — hovering in the air.

"Whooooa! What's this?" Replay cried.

Static stopped the magnetic beam, and Replay and the light crashed to the floor. Replay looked furious.

"Get him!" he ordered the clones.

Three of the Replay replicas charged at Static. Static aimed another beam at a metal cable on the floor. The cable sprung up, striking the three Re-plays. They all went sprawling.

Then Static flew across the studio and picked up Replay.

"This is where they tape *Finklestein's Monster*. I *like* that show. What is your problem?" Static asked.

"They axed *my* show for this piece of garbage," Replay snarled.

Static felt a hand tap his shoulder. He turned around to see his own duplicate staring at him. Before Static could react, the clone hit him with a Taser punch.

The punch sent Static flying. He crashed into one of the fake walls on the set.

Static rose to his feet. He was in a set designed to look like an office now. He could feel a bolt of energy sizzle past his face. Static quickly dodged and ducked behind a desk.

Static popped up. "Hey, clone clown. Catch!" he yelled.

Static tossed his flying disk at the clone. The clone ducked to avoid it. When he stood upright again, Static tackled him.

But the other Static was fast. He jumped to his feet and blasted Static with a charge of static electricity. Static flew against the wall, trapped by the energy.

Replay walked up to the Static look-alike.

"How does it feel, buddy, now that nobody likes you anymore?" Replay asked.

"Why are you doing this?" Static asked.

Replay scowled. "It's the network's fault. They ruined my life!"

"Get over it, man," Static said. "You're gonna trash the whole building 'cause they canceled your old show?"

Replay nodded. "You bet! And the beauty part is, when we're through, the whole world will think *you* did it!"

Static struggled to break free of the charge. He couldn't let Replay get away with it!

Replay grinned. "Now it's time to cancel *you,* Static!"

Suddenly, a voice rang through the studio. "Are you sure you want to do that on national television?"

Static couldn't believe it. It was Richie's voice! Replay turned around.

A remote-controlled camera wheeled up toward Replay. The red light blinking on it meant the camera was running.

Replay looked thrilled. "I-I-I'm on TV again?" he asked. Then his face changed. "Wait. No. Ruuuun!"

The Replay clones made a dash for the exit. The Static clone looked around, confused.

Static saw his chance. He nailed his replica with a Taser punch.

"Back at ya, copycat!" Static cried.

The Static clone was charged with energy. He flew across the stage and slammed into Replay.

There was a sizzling sound as the clone shocked Replay. Replay groaned and sank to the ground. In an instant, all of the energy clones vanished.

At that moment, Chief Barnstable burst through the room with several police officers. They surrounded Replay.

The chief smiled at Static. "We saw the whole thing on the jumbo TV screen outside, Static," he said. "It's a good thing someone was filming you."

Static smiled back. He was glad, too. He flew up to the camera control booth and found Richie walking out.

"Sure I'm not the evil twin?" Static asked.

"Yup," Richie teased. "The evil twin's better looking."

"When I asked for help with the ShockVox, you had your doubts, didn't you?" Static asked.

Richie nodded.

"Then why'd you help?" Static asked.

"I just went with my gut," Richie said. "And that was the right call."

Static and Richie walked down the hallway. Static felt pretty good. It was bad enough having everyone in Dakota City think he had gone bad, but the worst thing was not having Richie to count on. He was glad his friend hadn't given up on him.

"Speaking of guts," Static said, "how about some cheesesteaks? On me?"

Richie smiled. "You're buying? Maybe you are the clone after all!"